ACKNOWLEDGEMENTS:

My deepest gratitude to...

God Almighty for giving me the strength and courage to do this work

The Holy Prophet Muhammad (P.B.U.H) and his family for their light and guidance

My parents for their love, prayers and sacrifices

Rizwan, my soul mate and the greatest blessing in my life

Kamaal, Hadi, Hamza and Mokhtar, my princes in shining armor

Masuma, my sister, my joy and the best part of me

My publisher, Tehseen, for her friendship, patience, vision and sincerity

Shahraiz, for his creativity, insight and hard work

Fatema Kermalli for her eagle eye and all those who proofread and contributed

My family, relatives and friends for their unwavering support and encouragement

Nargis aunty and her green parrot Pepe who gave me so much happiness in my childhood

Orphans around the world who face the world with bravery and faith; you were my inspiration

In memory of my late father Abbas Parpia

Long ago, the kingdom of Lusitania sat hidden deep within the lush highlands of Hispania. It was a land filled with riches, peace and prosperity.

King Tariq and Queen Fatimah ruled the kingdom with kindness and equality. They were ready to welcome a new baby who would one day lead their kingdom.

Nine months later, a beautiful baby girl was born, with sparkling green eyes, rosy cheeks and curly tufts of ebony hair. She quickly reached out and grasped the queen's finger.

"We shall name her Siyana," said the queen happily. "She will protect our kingdom from harm."

As the king and queen embraced their baby, Shargor the Chief Advisor lurked nearby. Once again, he was planning something very evil and this time he knew he had to succeed. The long-desired Kingdom of Lusitania would soon be his to rule.

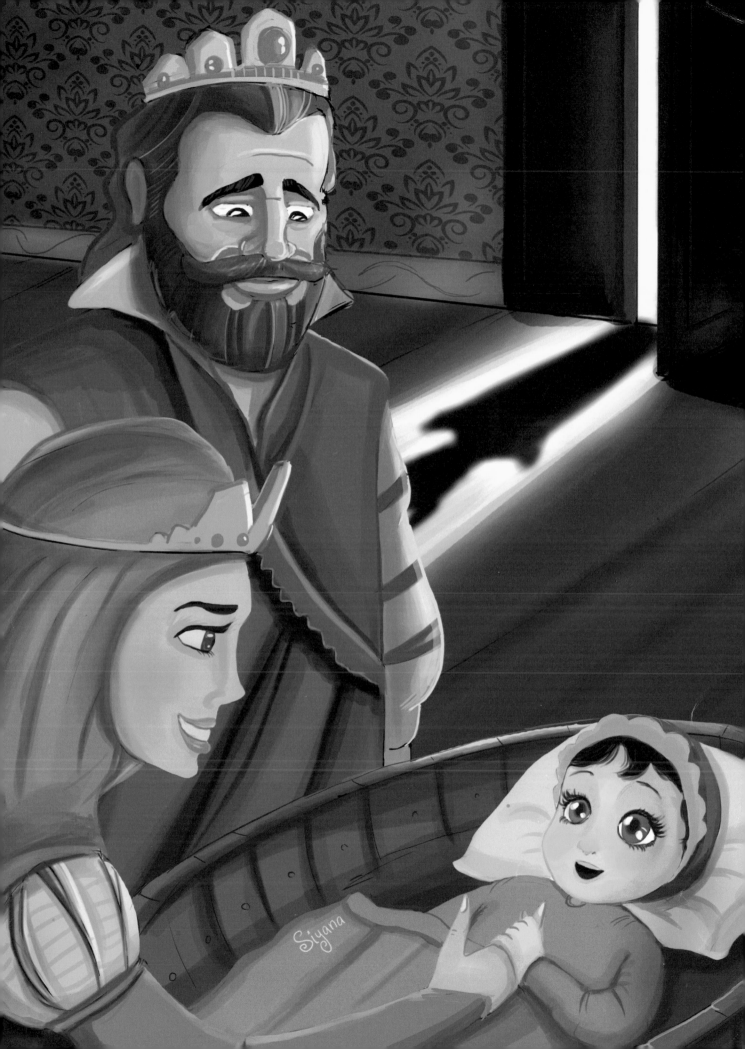

One night, as Siyana slept peacefully in her bassinet, Shargor unlocked the door and tiptoed carefully into the princess's nursery. In the dark of the night, he snatched the baby and hid her under his black cloak, hurrying swiftly out of the castle.

Shargor rode for hours in his chariot as the princess cried for her mother. It was dawn when the chariot finally came to a screeching halt. Shargor had ridden beyond the outskirts of Lusitania, and had entered the mountainous kingdom of Baetica.

He left the princess on the barren ground and hastily sped off, whipping his horse and cackling wickedly. "The king and queen shall be ruined, Mwahahaha!" he said.

Back at the castle, King Tariq and Queen Fatimah frantically searched for their baby.

"Where is my Siyana?" wailed the queen. "Where is my baby?" She ran back and forth, looking everywhere and asking everyone. King Tariq sent out a search party and announced a large reward for anyone who would find her.

Shargor arrived just in time, pretending to help find the princess. "I will lead the search party," he said, placing his bony fingers on the king's shoulder and puffing out his chest. "Don't worry, she will be found!"

But Shargor knew the princess would never be found and his evil plan was finally working. He was ready to take Lusitania into his own hands.

Meanwhile, a traveler on foot spotted a tiny baby on the desert ground. As he approached closer, he realized she laid still, her eyes closed and her lips parched.

He splashed some water on her face and after some time, her eyes fluttered. He was overjoyed! He picked her up and noticed an embroidered name on her pink blanket.

"Siyana" he read aloud. "What a beautiful name!" He poured some water into her mouth and carried her into Baetica.

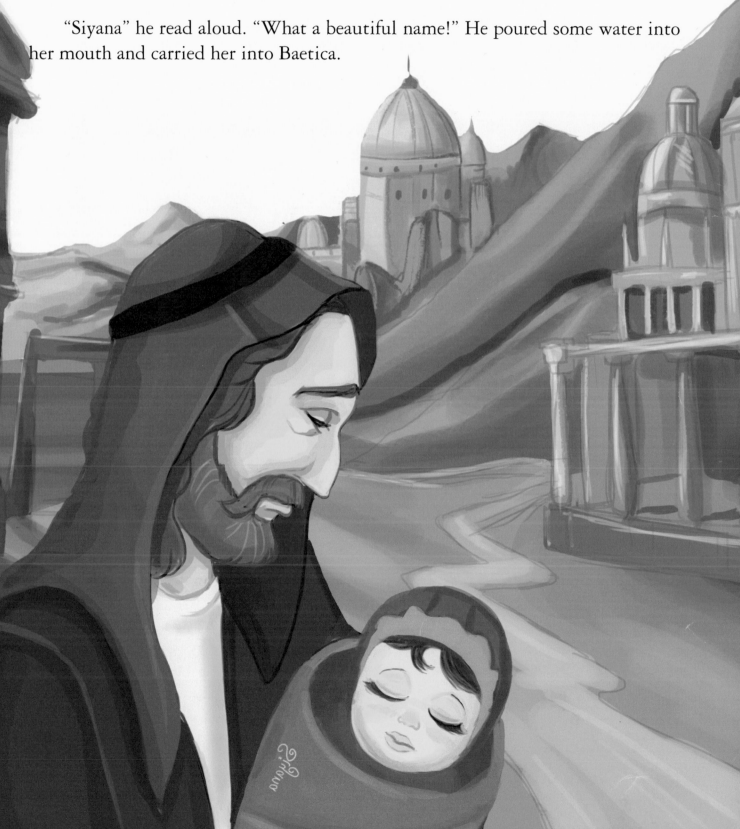

Days turned into nights and nights turned into weeks. The king and queen still had not found Siyana and their worries grew by day. King Tariq could not rule his kingdom well and kept making mistakes. Queen Fatimah stayed in her room all day and wept.

The king let Shargor make all of his decisions, giving him a lot of power. "I need to take some time off, Shargor" said the king. "Clear my mind a little. I entrust you to handle everything in my absence."

Shargor smiled from ear to ear. He had gotten what he wanted.

A few months later, Shargor had gained so much power and money that he began to control everything in Lusitania. The entire kingdom was tricked into obeying him.

Shargor imprisoned King Tariq and Queen Fatimah in the castle's dungeons and those that spoke out against his crimes were punished.

Sixteen years later, Siyana had grown up to be a beautiful young girl at El Sol Orphanage for Girls in the kingdom of Baetica. She was tall and graceful, with large twinkling green eyes and a heartwarming smile.

Siyana had become a favorite at the orphanage. She was always helping out as much as she could, especially with the younger children. She would play soccer wearing her long dress in the daytime, knit in the evenings, and read books at night. Her willful personality was loved by everyone, especially the Head Caretaker Ms. Salma.

As pretty as Siyana was, she would always wear her hijab to cover herself when she went out, and had done so since she was nine years old. She would often go to the market with Ms. Salma to get food for the orphans. They would both wear a long scarf to protect themselves and look respectful. Ms. Salma had taught her that "true beauty shines from the heart when you are with God".

Although Siyana kept busy throughout the day, she would always look forward to writing letters with Pepe, her little parrot. At ten years old, she had looked after Pepe when his wing was injured outside the orphanage. He was a tropical bird with brilliant red, yellow and blue feathers.

One sunny morning, Pepe the parrot shrieked merrily as he saw Siyana skipping into the orphanage from the market.

"Pepe want cookie! Pepe want cookie!" he said.

Siyana reached into her bag and pulled out delicious, chocolate-covered coconut macaroons, Pepe's favorite treat. She stretched out her hand and he instantly helped himself, munching on them happily. These macaroons were quite expensive, so Siyana could only afford to buy them a few times a year for her favorite bird.

"What shall we write today?" asked Siyana, pulling out her pen and paper onto a desk next to the window. Pepe made himself comfortable on her shoulder, squawking in delight as he savored his macaroons.

When Siyana was very young, Ms. Salma had taught all the girls at the orphanage about the All Knowing and Most Merciful God. She had told them that even though He was the Great Creator and Master of the Universe, He always listened and helped anyone that called on Him. Ms. Salma had given all the girls special pens to use as a way to connect with God.

"My dear sweet girls" Ms. Salma had said, "During our prayers, we speak to our Lord with beautiful words and we praise Him and thank Him for all that He has given us. But true connection to God is to have Him in our hearts all the time, remembering Him and trusting in Him. One way to do this is by writing letters to Him on any day, at any time. This is your special time to tell Him in your own words how you feel, your worries, your joys and what you need. When we tell Him everything that is in our hearts, we feel better because He loves us so much and is always there for us. So go on, put your trust in Him."

The girls would eagerly wait for the time of week when they would write letters to God and send it off into the lake with the hope that their prayers would come true.

"Squarrrrk!" Pepe shrieked as he gobbled up his last macaroon.

Siyana realized she had been daydreaming for half an hour! As she observed the hustle and bustle of the town outside her window, Siyana thought about what she was going to write. She peered curiously at her blank paper.

"Today I'm going to pray for others" said Siyana with a nod. "God loves it when we think of others before ourselves!"

Oh my Lord, my Guide, my Everything,
How I've missed you, even though I talked to you just an hour ago in my Salaah! I am so grateful for everything You have blessed me with and ask that You always look after everyone I love. Today, I have an extra special request. I would like for you to help other people, those who are sick, poor, and oppressed. They really need your help, more than I want a new dress or more than Pepe wants his macaroons! I have heard that the Kingdom of Lusitania really needs you. The people there are starving and getting very sick. I know you will listen to my prayer and will help them.

With much love,
Your beloved Siyana

Siyana dipped her pen into the fresh ink and began to write, only stopping now and then deep in thought. Once finished, she sealed her scroll with a kiss and tied it to Pepe's feet. He flew out the window, as he did every day, and released the letter into the lake.

Early next morning, as Siyana swept the kitchen floor, Ms. Salma barged in, her cheeks flushed with excitement. "Siyana" she said slowly, taking some deep breaths calming herself. "We're going to visit Baetica Academy, your dream school!"

Siyana stood in silence, stunned.

"I sent them some of your work and they thought you were very bright! They want to see you first thing tomorrow." Siyana was overjoyed! She always had a passion for knowledge, and Baetica Academy was the top school in the kingdom.

"Wow, nothing is impossible," Siyana said. "The important thing is to always try your best and put your trust in God!"

The next day, Siyana slipped on her velvet green dress with shiny gold buttons. It was quite plain, but she loved it all the more for its simplicity. She saved this dress for all her special occasions, and rightfully so. It made her look very smart and matched her sparkling green eyes. She tied her black wavy hair into a bun and wore a long scarf.

"Why wear such a pretty dress if no one can see your hair?" little Maryam asked as she admired Siyana.

"My sweet Maryam," Siyana replied. "You don't have to look pretty for other people. Just as we wouldn't judge a book by its cover, we shouldn't judge people by the way they look. What is on the inside and the way you act is much more important. Hijab reminds us that we should have an outstanding character."

Little Maryam nodded. "God is very happy when we wear our hijab!" she said. With that, she flashed her charming smile, gave Siyana a kiss on the cheek and pranced away happily.

After what seemed like hours of riding in their carriage, Ms. Salma and Siyana finally arrived at Baetica Academy in the outskirts of the kingdom. As they dismounted the cart, a harsh gust of wind swept them off their feet.

"Whoa!" cried Ms. Salma.

Just then, the wind began to encircle them, collecting clouds of dust and grass.

It kept forming and collecting more speed, destroying everything that came in its path.

"Run Siyana!" Ms. Salma screamed. "It's a tornado! You have to run!"

"I can't leave you!" yelled Siyana over the roaring wind. But soon, she had no choice. Everyone was running in different directions. She picked herself up and ran faster than she ever had, not looking back even once.

"Eek!" squealed Siyana, bolting upright, chattering her teeth. "That was cold!"

The sun had just dawned and an elderly couple was standing in front of her, a bucket of ice cold water in their hands. "We needed to wake you up" they said together.

"Where am I?" Siyana asked, rubbing her eyes.

"Well, for starters, you're in Lusitania!" said the old man, grinning and revealing several missing teeth. "I'm Jamil and—"I'm Layla," interrupted the old lady standing next to him. They stood there silently, waiting patiently and smiling.

"Oh! Why yes, I'm Siyana!" said Siyana, quickly standing up and brushing the dirt off her now scruffy green dress.

"My, what an... interesting name," Layla said hesitantly. "Are you named after the Missing Princess Siyana?"

"Missing princess? Uh, I don't think so. I'm from Baetica. There was a storm and I had to run," Siyana said, looking down and remembering Ms. Salma, Pepe and everyone at the orphanage.

"You shouldn't mention your name to anyone here." Jamil stuttered, his forehead dripping with sweat. "Our ruler Shargor has forbidden it."

"Why is that?" Siyana asked curiously.

"It was sixteen years ago," Layla whispered, "Queen Fatimah and King Tariq had a baby girl named Siyana. Under their rule, Lusitania was such a wonderful place filled with life and color. When Princess Siyana was captured just days after her birth, King Tariq lost his bearing and Shargor took over."

Layla looked around to make sure no one was listening and leaned in closer.

"Now look what he has done to our land!" she cried, her voice still hushed. "People are suffering and injustice is everywhere. King Tariq and Queen Fatima have been imprisoned ever since."

Siyana's eyes twinkled. Her heart began to pound. Could it be possible? Were the king and queen her parents? Surely it was an outrageous idea, but there was only one way she could know for sure. She had to go to the castle and find out!

That night, after a simple dinner, Siyana sat to write yet another letter with her special pen, a candle flickering by her side.

"To my beloved God who watches over me and protects me,

I rely on You and trust in You, for You have promised to answer anyone who calls on You! I write to You in a time of need and confusion. I am here, all alone in a foreign place with the kindness of strangers. They have nothing, yet they share their food and home with me. Please bless them and reward them greatly. I have never known where I came from and what my true purpose is. I am going to the castle tomorrow and the journey will be very dangerous. Please guide me and help me! With your help, I know I can do anything.

All my love, Siyana."

Siyana kissed the letter as her tears splotched the paper. She instinctively reached out for Pepe, but realized he wasn't there. She then remembered Ms. Salma had taught her that although God loves to hear from us through duas and letters, it is more important to always remember Him in our hearts. It is when our hearts are connected to Him that we find peace. She prayed that everyone she loved was safe and folded the letter into her dress pocket.

Early next morning, Siyana bid farewell to Jamil and Layla.

"Don't go!" Layla sobbed. Jamil, too proud to show his tears, turned away and waved goodbye. Siyana promised she would visit them both soon.

"I'm lending my Habeeba to you," Jamil said "She is the only thing of value that I own and I will never sell her." He brought out a beautiful white mare from the shed. "This way you will have to come to see us again."

Siyana mounted Habeeba, clicked her tongue, and kicked her legs. They were off to the Grand Castle of Lusitania! Siyana could not help but notice the lack of greenery Lusitania's highlands were once known for. "Whatever this Shargor has done must be awful. This place looks so dreary" she muttered to herself.

As they galloped over muddy roads and barren fields, Siyana felt something flutter onto her shoulder. She looked to her side, and to her surprise, it was Pepe!

"Pepe!" Siyana cried in delight, almost falling over. "How did you find me?"

"Pepe want cookie!" Pepe squawked, looking just as glad. "Pepe want cookie!"

"I really have to teach you something new!" Siyana said, giggling. "Thank you God! You are the best! You always help me every step of the way! Pepe, boy am I glad to see you!"

Siyana pulled on the reins as they approached the castle and Habeeba halted. She swiftly dismounted the horse and hid behind a tree. Hundreds of guards surrounded the castle. Siyana's breath quickened and her hands began to tremble. How was she ever going to get inside?

Siyana noticed an opening in the back, and she grabbed at the opportunity. She whispered into Habeeba's ears and the horse galloped towards the soldiers, distracting them for a brief second.

Running at full speed, Siyana managed to get inside the half open gate when she heard the guards coming in after her. She didn't know where the path would lead, but she had no choice except to follow.

It was extremely dark in the tunnel. Squinting her eyes, Siyana tried to make out her path, but she still could not see a thing. Water dripped from above and mice scurried past her feet below. Suddenly, the dungeon became brighter. Pepe's tropical colors were reflecting against the water!

"There they are!" a guard bellowed, motioning his comrades towards Pepe's direction. Siyana gulped.

"Pepe, I need you to distract them now!" Siyana whispered, wide-eyed.

Pepe flew in the other direction and the guard went running behind him. With the little light she had left flickering behind her, Siyana tread the dark passageway that lay in front.

In the pitch black darkness, Siyana grew frightened. "I am not alone" she said aloud, assuring herself. "God is always with me."

She noticed several bolted doors and began calling for the king or queen, hoping someone would answer quickly.

"I'm looking for the king and queen!" Siyana shouted desperately. "Is anyone in there?"

A graceful woman came to one of the doors, and a frail man with graying hair stood beside her. They looked pale and tired, but she felt as though she knew them.

The woman's eyes widened instantly. "Those twinkling green eyes!" she said, pointing to Siyana and looking back at the man. "I recognize them! It's my Siyana! I knew she was still alive!" She sobbed with joy, reaching for Siyana's hand through the metal bars.

Siyana examined the queen curiously. It was as if she was looking at an older reflection! She took out her name piece from her pocket and gave it to the queen.

"This is from your blanket when you were just a baby!" said Queen Fatimah, tears streaming down her face. "All thanks to God Almighty, my Siyana has returned!"

Siyana was so happy, she could barely feel her hands! She unlocked the door as fast as she could with her special pen. The king and queen were finally free.

Just then, hundreds of guards stormed the dungeon in an attempt to capture the king and queen. Siyana bravely stood in their way.

"Why do you attempt to imprison them?" she asked. "Do you know who they are? These are my parents, the king and queen of Lusitania, chosen by their people to serve in their best interests. They have ruled this land with nothing but fairness and kindness, and you want to lock them away? How can you fear Shargor, who is only a man, when you should fear your God, the One who created us all!"

To her amazement, the guards bowed their heads in shame and made way for the king and queen. Shargor was immediately dethroned from power and put to trial. When he saw Siyana from afar, he looked downcast and ashamed, tears pouring from his eyes. He realized that it is God who has the true power, and he would have to answer to Him for his evil actions. Shargor fell to the ground and sobbed into his hands, pleading to God for forgiveness.

"Send him away" growled the king, "he has brought much harm to the kingdom and our family."

Siyana approached Shargor, who was bent over in a pitiful state. "It is never too late to ask forgiveness from God" she said to him.

Siyana looked at her parents, who were startled by what she had just said. "Forgiveness is the path to greatness," she said. "God, the Most Merciful is always there for us, even when we have done something terribly wrong. He keeps the doors of forgiveness open and we can turn to Him and speak to Him anytime"

Meanwhile, Jamil and Layla had told some villagers that Siyana the princess may have returned and word spread quickly. Masses of people gathered outside the castle waiting eagerly to see what had happened.

King Tariq and Queen Fatimah walked out into the balcony with Princess Siyana by their side and announced to the people the return of their daughter. The crowds cheered joyously, rose petals decorated the kingdom and its people were hopeful once again.

When all her friends from the orphanage came to visit, including Ms. Salma and Little Maryam, Siyana told them the tale of her journey and how she learned that God has a plan for everyone. Through Princess Siyana's kind heart and generous nature, the castle was turned into an orphanage, school and library.

With so much joy and contentment bursting from her chest, Siyana remembered that it was her trust and love for God that made her happy. "Everything I have is from God. The kingdoms of the Heavens and the Earth truly belong to Him and His reign has no end," she said. "So everything I do will be for Him too InshaAllah".

In her new bedroom, Siyana pressed her forehead to the ground and thanked God for bringing her back to her family once again.

Pepe's Coconut Macaroons

Pepe loves sweet treats. Bake a batch of one of his favorite snack—miniature chocolate macaroons! "Squarrrrk!"

Ingredients

2 cups shredded coconut
½ cup sweetened condensed milk
1 tsp vanilla extract
12 ounces semi-sweet chocolate chips, melted

Directions

Preheat oven to 350 degrees F (180 degrees C). Combine coconut and milk.
Add vanilla and mix well. Drop from teaspoon, 1 inch apart, onto waxed paper.
Bake in oven for 10 minutes or until delicately browned.
Remove from sheet at once. Dip them in delicious chocolate.

Ask an adult to help you bake these delicious treats

My Letter to God

Help Princess Siyana find her way back home!

Published by Sun Behind The Cloud Publications Ltd, PO Box 15889, Birmingham, B16 6NZ

This edition first published in 2015

A CIP Catalogue record of this book is available from the British Library

ISBN: 978-1-908110-27-5 (Paperback)

www.sunbehindthecloud.com